Tweedle Dee Dee

CHARLOTTE VOAKE

WALKER BOOKS
AND SUBSIDIARIES

LONDON • BOSTON • SYDNEY • AUCKLAND

ONCE in a wood
there was
a tree,

the finest tree
you ever did
see.

And the green
leaves grew
around around
around,

the green leaves
grew around.

AND
on that tree
there was
a branch,
the finest branch
you ever
did see.

The branch was
on the tree,
the tree was in
the wood,
and the green
leaves grew
around
around around,
the green leaves
grew around.

AND on that branch there was a nest, the finest nest you ever did see.

The nest was on
the branch,

the branch was on
the tree,

the tree was in
the wood,

and the green
leaves grew around
around around,
the green leaves
grew around.

AND in that nest there were some eggs, the finest little eggs you ever did see.

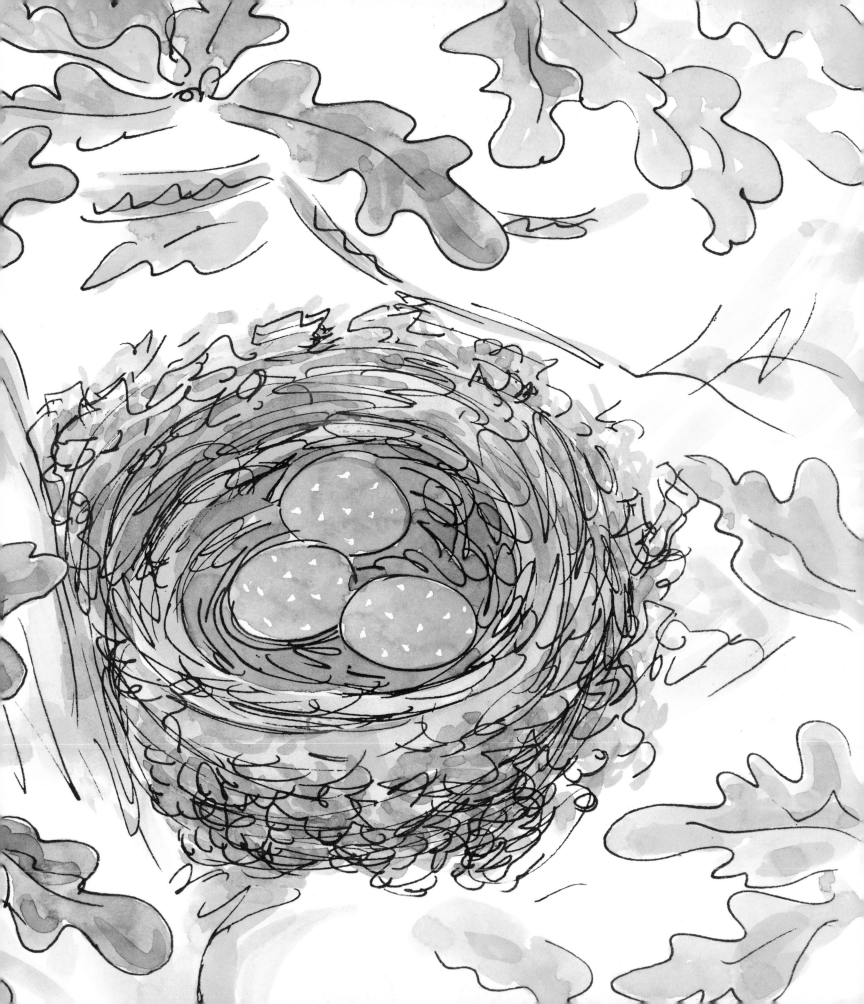

The eggs were
in the nest,

the nest was
on the branch,

the branch
was on the tree,

the tree was in
the wood,

and the green leaves
grew around around
around, the green
leaves grew around.

AND in those
eggs
there were some
birds,

ONE and TWO

and THREE!

"CHEEP!" went one.
"CHEEP!" went another,
and the third went,

"TWEEDLE
DEE DEE!"

The birds were in
the eggs,

the eggs were in
the nest,

the nest was on
the branch,

the branch was
on the tree,

the tree was
in the wood ...

and the green leaves grew
around around around.
And the birds went

"TWEEDLE
DEE DEE!"

THE TREE SONG

Once i-n a wood there was a tree, the fi - nest tree you ev-er did see, and the

green leaves grew a - round a-round a-round, and the green leaves grew a - round. And

o - n th-at tree there was a branch, the fi - nest branch you

Charlotte Voake

The work of Charlotte Voake is renowned throughout the world for its gentle wit, quiet observation, airy exuberance and charm. Winner of the **Smarties Book Prize** for *Ginger,* Charlotte says of her work, *"I just draw with ink, over and over again – until I think, 'Aha, that's how it should be!'"*

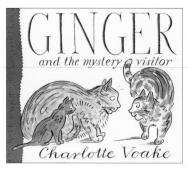

ISBN 978-1-4063-2238-5

ISBN 978-1-4063-1269-0

ISBN 978-1-4063-1270-6

ISBN 978-0-7445-8958-0

ISBN 978-1-4063-0523-4

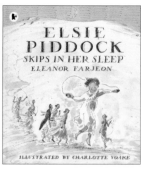

ISBN 978-1-4063-1405-2

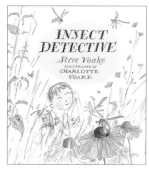

ISBN 978-1-4063-1051-1

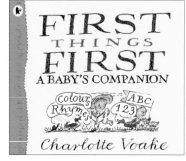

ISBN 978-1-4063-1272-0

ISBN 978-1-4063-1271-3

Available from all good bookstores

www.walker.co.uk